PAULA DAN...

I, AMBER BROWN

Illustrated by Tony Ross

BL:3.7 Points:2.0

#32746

A
LITTLE APPLE
PAPERBACK

SCHOLASTIC INC.

New York Toronto London Auckland Sydney
Mexico City New Delhi Hong Kong Buenos Aires

To Elizabeth Levy

No part of this publication may be reproduced in whole or in part, or stored in a retrieval system, or transmitted in any form or by any means, electronic, mechanical, photocopying, recording, or otherwise, without written permission of the publisher. For information regarding permission, write to G.P. Putnam's Sons, an imprint of Penguin Putnam Books for Young Readers, a division of Penguin Group (USA) Inc., 345 Hudson Street, New York, NY 10014.

ISBN 0-439-07169-0

23 22 21 20 19   5 6 7 8 9/0

Printed in the U.S.A.   40

Chapter One

. . . Only fourteen more days until Christmas.

. . . Only twelve more days until Christmas vacation.

. . . Only a few more minutes before I, Amber Brown, collapse from shopping exhaustion.

I, Amber Brown, am too pooped to pop.

"Too pooped to pop" is what I, Amber Brown, say when I am absolutely exhausted.

And I am totally exhausted . . . . but not quite ready to quit because I have to find a few more presents.

I, Amber Brown, am not only running out of energy . . . . . I am running out of money.

It's a good thing that I will be making some of my presents, but there is still one more that I need to find and buy.

"Amber, this bookstore, as much as I love bookstores, has got to be the last place we go today. I am shopped out. I am wiped out. I am just not used to this," Max, my mom's fiancé and my future stepdad, says.

I can tell that he is also too pooped to pop.

I smile at him. "Christmas shopping is *almost* done."

". . . . . And your Hanukkah shopping too." Max grins back.

I, Amber Brown, am used to Christmas shopping . . . now with Max in our lives, I'm going to be getting used to Hanukkah shopping too.

Hanukkah . . . that really added to my list

. . . eight days of giving presents to Max
. . . . and he's going to give me eight days
of presents too.

I, Amber Brown, could get used to this
. . . . *will* get used to this because Max and
Mom have decided that we will celebrate
all of our holidays . . . . actually, I say celebrate . . . they say honor . . . . either way it's
a good deal, the way I see it.

Max's presents are already hidden in my
closet. I got those when I went out shopping with Mom the other day.

Now I've been getting presents for my
mom and for some other people.

I got Christmas presents for my mom . . .
and some Hanukkah ones too.

Max is going to bring a menorah over to
our house . . . and every night that he's visiting and it's Hanukkah, we're going to light
the candles.

"Ouch," Max says, as he drops a package
on his foot. "Now my feet are really aching."

"You only dropped it on one foot so stop complaining," I tease him. "Anyway, it's not like it's bowling balls. It's the soccer ball for Justin and the basketball for his little brother, Danny."

"It's going to be fun to wrap those presents." Max laughs.

"Garbage bags," I say. "Medium-sized green garbage bags tied with red ribbon and giant red bows . . . that's how I'm going to do it. They're boys . . . and boys don't care about how a present is wrapped. I could wrap it in toilet paper, and they wouldn't care."

Max makes a face. "Well, that's a generalization if I ever heard one. If I said something like that about girls . . . . you and your mom would nail me."

I bite my lip. "Ooops, sorry, Max. . . . . I guess I better ask you something. Does this mean that you care about how your presents are wrapped . . . . because if you do, this means I'm going to have to take the toilet paper off them and wrap them up again."

There's a funny look on his face like he's not sure what to say.

I decide to take him out of his misery and tell him the truth.

After all, I've almost shopped him to death, he's got a damaged foot, and he's not used to holiday shopping with a fourth-grade girl.

So I say, "It's a joke, Max. . . . I wrapped your presents normally."

Max smiles. "Amber, I would love the presents wrapped any way because they came from you."

"I was just joking though. I'm just a joke-ster sometimes," I say, and then look over at a special table that says GIFTS FOR YOUR TEACHER.

Max pretends to frown about my being a jokester.

Over the loud speaker is the sound of Christmas music.

It's "Santa Claus Is Coming to Town."

I start to sing. . . . . "You better watch out. . . . You better not pout. . . . . Santa Claus is coming to town."

Max joins in and sings along with me.

He actually sings in tune.

Some people are looking at us and smil-ing.

Some are laughing.

Some join in.

After the song is finished, Max grins at me. "You know, Amber . . . I think that this is going to be the best holiday of my life . . . . spending time with you and Sarah."

I grin back. Now that I'm getting used to the fact that Mom and Max are going to get married, and that my Mom and Dad aren't going to get back together again, I grin at Max a lot.

It's like he's been a part of my life for a long time, not just since I got back from visiting England last summer with my Aunt

Pam . . . the trip when I didn't get to go to Paris to see my dad because I got the chicken pox.

Then I think about my dad. I remember Christmases from when he and my mom were still married. Some of them were happy.

I'm glad that this is going to be the best Christmas of Max's life . . . . for me, it's going to be a little weird. With Dad just back from living in Paris, I'm worried that there are going to be some problems for me, just like there were at Thanksgiving. I know the deal is that I spend Christmas with my mom, but I also know that I'm going to be able to spend some time over the rest of the vacation with my dad. But since my dad doesn't have his own place yet, I'll be able to live at home and just visit with Dad . . . . unless he takes me into New York City like he did at Thanksgiving.

I, Amber Brown, am going to have to get used to all of this. Even though my parents haven't lived together for a long time, this is just the beginning of their joint custody deal . . . . and sometimes the stuff that's happening does not make me happy.

Max repeats, "This will be the best holiday of my life. . . . . And I want it to be very special for you too. . . . Our first Hanukkah-Christmas together."

I say, "Thanks," and then I look over at the table.

There are a gazillion books there . . . and teacher mugs . . . and stationery . . . and bookmarks. . . . . And then I see it . . . the perfect, perfect book for Mrs. Holt. It's a guide to the twelve months of the year . . . holidays, special occasions, fun class projects.

I, Amber Brown, love this book, and I just know that Mrs. Holt is going to LOVE this book too.

"I hope that no one else gives this to her," I say to Max. "And I hope that she loans it to me."

Max puts down all of his packages and looks at the book with me. "This is a great choice . . . . there are activities . . . and recipes. This is terrific."

I hug the book to me. "I just love facts like this."

"Would you like a copy of this book for yourself?" Max asks.

"Even though I'm not a teacher? Oh yes, it's so much fun. And each day we see each other, I'll tell you the fact of the day."

"Then I'll get it for you," Max says.

"Thank you. Thank you. Thank you." I smile at him again. "Is this going to be for a Christmas present or for a Hanukkah present? Because Hanukkah is sooner."

"It's for today . . . . December 11," he says.

I look in the book. "On December 11, 1918, the first U.S. monument to an insect was dedicated in Alabama. It was to the boll weevil."

"Well," Max says, "that's definitely a day to celebrate."

When I, Amber Brown, get home, I'm going to immediately write to Justin, who moved to Alabama . . . and tell him this fact. It will definitely drive him buggy.

Justin Daniels. . . . This is going to be the first Christmas that he and I aren't going to spend part of the day together.

This holiday is definitely going to be a time of firsts . . . . the first time that Max will be part of it, the first time that Justin and his family won't be part of it, and the first time in two years that my father will be around for Christmas . . . and he won't be part of it.

That's definitely a lot of parts! And I just hope that those parts won't be a whole lot of trouble. . . . . . 'Tis the season to be jolly . . . . I just hope that everyone keeps re-membering that.

Chapter
Two

"Deck the halls with poison ivy," I, Amber Brown, sing off-tune.

"Fa, la, la, la, la, la, la, la, la." My mom also sings off-tune.

Aunt Pam, my mom's sister, says that none of us can carry a tune in a bucket.

Actually, I have never seen anyone carry a tune in a bucket.

"We fish you a Merry Christmas . . . we fish you a Merry Christmas." My mom holds up a charm with a fish on it.

Maybe with that fish, even though we

can't carry a tune in a bucket, we can carry a tuna in a bucket.

I, Amber Brown, love to pun.

I also love to make presents for my friends for the holidays.

B . . . R . . . A . . . N . . . D . . . I

I pick out the beads to go between the letters . . . . and the charms to go on the bracelet . . . . a little dog charm that looks like her dog (except that there is no slobber coming out of the charm dog's mouth) . . . . a nail polish bottle charm, to remind her of the time we painted our nails . . . and the dog's nails too . . .

For my Aunt Pam, I make a name bracelet with the letters P . . . A . . . M . . . E . . . L . . . A. She'd have to have a miniature wrist if I only wrote P . . . A . . . M. I put charms on it . . . a book, because she teaches English, a Big Ben building because she loves England, and a bunch of ant charms

. . . because, after all, she is an aunt. . . . .

For Brenda, my Ambersitter, I also make a name bracelet. I add cooking charms—a pot, a pan, and teeny-tiny spatula. (I picked those charms as a joke because Brenda is the weirdest, if not the worstest, cook ever.) I also add a pair of scissors because Brenda always cuts her hair strangely . . . so strangely that my mom once made Brenda promise that she would NEVER cut my hair . . . . or pierce any part of my body. . . . I am glad that mom said that about my hair but I RE- ALLY wish that she would let me get my ears pierced . . . but she says I can't, not until I'm twelve.

I finish working on the alphabet and charm bracelets and start working on the Scrabble jewelry. (For months, mom and I have been going to garage, house, and rum- mage sales, buying up all of the old Scrab- ble games that we could find. Now we are ready to use the tiles.)

I pick up an "O" and then an "H" tile. They're for my teacher, Olivia Holt. If she wears them one way, so that the "O" is on her right ear . . . she'll spell out "OH". . . . if she wears the "H" on her right ear, she'll spell out HO . . . which is very Christmas . . . especially if you say it several times.

Then, I make a pair for Aunt Pam . . . but the tiles aren't "A" and "P." They are "P" and "T" (for Thompson).

I'm almost done.

I look over at my mom, who is making sure that all the rhinestones are sticking on the picture frame that I made for my Grandma Brown, my dad's mom.

I haven't seen Grandma Brown, who lives in Florida, since before my Dad left for Paris.

It makes me sad, but maybe now that my Dad is back, we can go visit her sometime.

I take a plain picture frame and start putting rhinestones and pearls on it. When it's all finished, I'll put one of my pictures in it. (And I'll put rhinestones on the picture.)

My mom says, "This is fun . . . and it saves money."

I nod. With what I borrowed from my mom, I don't think that I'll be getting any allowance again until the middle of March. If I weren't making some of the presents, I doubt that I would be getting an allowance again until August.

I start working on one of Max's presents.

It's a salt and pepper shaker set that I found at the 99 Cent store, and I am putting lots of rhinestones on it.

I think that it will make Max smile.

I show my mother. "Isn't this the perfect gift for a bowling coach? I know that I won't strike out with this item."

First, my mom groans at my pun . . . and maybe even the thought of rhinestone bowling-ball-and-pin salt and pepper shakers, and then says, "He'll be so grateful that you could spare the time to make this for him."

I work on Max's gift.

I know that it's sort of tacky, but it's fun.

On the bowling pin, I glue on rhinestones in the shape of a strike, X.

On the bowling ball, I start to make a rhinestone slash,/, like a spare.

My mom looks at it and says, "When I look at those shakers, I think about how they are going to be back here when Max and I get married, and we all live together."

I close my eyes for a minute while I think about what she's said.

I know that they are engaged.

I know that they are going to get married.

I just have trouble thinking about all of us living together.

While my eyes are closed, disaster strikes!

"Oooops," I say, opening my eyes.

The glue has escaped from the sides of the tube and is on my hand.

My fingers are glued together. So are the bowling ball and the tube of glue . . . . all attached to my left hand.

This is not good.

In fact, it's pretty bad.

I go to wipe my eyes with my left hand but my mother grabs it, quickly.

"Don't touch your eyes," she warns.

I don't.

Her hand, which is holding mine, is now stuck to my hand, to the bowling ball and to the tube of glue.

"This is a very sticky situation," I say.

"Not funny," she says, and then starts laughing.

I start laughing too.

"I wonder if this is what people mean when they talk about mother-daughter bonding."

She shakes her head.

I think about mothers and daughters . . . . and then I think about fathers.

"Mom," I say. "Dad's going to be here to pick me up for dinner soon. Maybe we'll all have to go to dinner together."

Sometimes, even though I, Amber Brown, know that it's not a good idea . . . I still think about my parents getting back together.

The only way that I think that will happen is if I glue them together.

"Dinner together???!!!!" My mom shakes her head. "Don't even think about it. . . . THAT would be a *very* sticky situation. No, the less that I see of your father, the better."

I, Amber Brown, hate when my mom says things like that. It makes me feel really bad.

I used to think that my mom was practically perfect, but ever since she found out that my dad was moving back, she's been a little weird . . . . and sometimes she says mean things about him.

I hate when she does that.

"Nail polish remover. That's what we need," my mom says.

"I'll go get it," I volunteer and stand up.

My mother's hand moves when I do.

I realize that if I'm going to get the nail polish remover, it's going to be a mother-daughter activity.

I also realize that I have to go to the bathroom, which is not a mother-daughter activity, not at my age.

This is definitely going to become embarrassing if my mother and I remain this attached.

We go up the steps, hands glued together, to her makeup drawer.

Nail polish remover. . . .

It works.

I rush to the bathroom.

My mom goes downstairs. "Hurry up. Your father will be here any minute, and I really don't want him to be here any longer than he has to be."

While I'm upstairs, the phone rings.

I rush to get it.

It's for me.

It's Brandi, who says, "Bulletin. Bulletin. Bulletin. Do I have a bulletin for you!!!! It's so amazing. And you've just got to convince your mom to let you do it too. Guess. You've got to guess what it is."

I, Amber Brown, have no idea.

Chapter
Three

Brandi is sooooooooo excited. "You've got three guesses."

I don't know where to start. "You're going to Disneyland."

"No. Two more." She giggles.

"You're getting married to Fredric Allen," I say.

"Noooooooooooooooooo. Gross," she says. "I'm just going to have to tell you."

I, Amber Brown, knew that would make her tell me. Fredric Allen is the kid in our class who picks his nose, and sometimes even eats it. He also forgot to zip up his fly on the day the class pictures were taken.

"I'm going to get my ears pierced. My parents said that I could do it as a Christmas present . . . . and guess what? Kelly's parents said that she could get hers done too."

My stomach feels sick.

I want to cry.

Two of my friends are getting their ears pierced and I have to wait 'til I'm twelve.

That's over two years from now. It's not fair.

Brandi says, "Kelly and I are going to go over to the mall and get them done today. Amber, you've got to convince your mom to let you get them done now . . . . with us. Just tell her that our moms said yes."

I don't say anything for a minute.

Brandi says, "Do you think my mom should talk to your mom?"

I shake my head and then realize that Brandi can't see that on the phone. "No. My mom said I have to wait and anyway, my dad's picking me up soon."

"That's not fair." Brandi says. "Maybe your dad could take you."

"I have to ask my mom," I say. "Maybe I can get her to change her mind."

Just because my mom had to wait until she was seventeen to get her ears pierced doesn't mean that I have to wait until I'm twelve.

"Can't you beg her? Explain that *every-one* is getting pierced ears . . . or already has them," Brandi says. "Oh, please. It'll be so cool if we could all go to the mall today and get it done."

My head is really beginning to ache. There's no way that my mom is going to say yes . . . . and it seems that Brandi Colwin, one of my best friends in the whole entire world, and Kelly Green, the new kid in our class and our new friend, have already made plans to do something that they know that I'm not going to be able to do.

I was so happy until I got this call.

I wish that my dad had gotten here and taken me away before the phone call came.

I sigh. "I'll try. Gotta go. If I don't call you back in ten minutes you'll know that my mom won't let me do it."

"I'll cross my fingers . . . . and my toes." Brandi says. "It will be *totally* wonderful if you can do this too."

Hanging up, I rush into my bedroom and change into a top that doesn't have glue on it, and then I hurry downstairs, rubbing at a piece of glue that's still stuck to the top of my hand.

I go into the kitchen where my mom is cleaning up the stuff that I was making.

"Thanks for doing that," I say and start putting things away too. "Mom. I have something to ask you . . . . and please don't say no."

"What?" She gives me a suspicious look.

I speak very quickly. "Brandi and Kelly are getting their ears pierced today . . . . and they want me to go with them . . . . and get mine done too. Oh, please . . . . oh please . . . . . oh pretty please with sugar on top."

"No." She shakes her head. "I told you that you have to wait until you are twelve to get that done. . . . I want you to wait. . . . I need to see that you will be responsible enough to keep your ears from getting infected. Amber, you are not organized. You don't keep your room clean . . . .

27

and even if I do change my mind, it won't be until I've seen a great many reports about how well you are doing in school. I want you to show that you are being responsible."

"I promise," I say. "I promise to be good. I am being responsible now. My grades are really good lately. And I promise that I will keep my room organized and clean."

"After you have done all of that, I will think about it . . . . but not until then."

"Mom," I beg.

She shakes her head. "Case closed."

That's it.

I know my mother.

She's not going to let me do it.

I am so unhappy.

I start to cry . . . but that doesn't do any good.

My mom just keeps organizing things.

I look at the clock.

It's ten minutes after four.

It's past the time that I told Brandi that I would call if my mom said yes.

The doorbell rings.

It's my dad.

Too late to call Brandi. I bet that she and Kelly are already on the way to the mall.

He's not going to be very happy to see me this upset.

I take a deep breath, wipe my tears, and go answer the door.

"Honey, what's wrong?" he asks.

"I'll tell you later," I say.

My mother comes into the living room.

Her voice is soooo cold when she speaks. "Philip. Just make sure that Amber isn't out too late. She has homework to do."

He nods and then he looks at me. "You're wearing the sweatshirt we got in New York."

It's the one that my dad bought for me at Thanksgiving and on it, the writing says, "JUST BE GLAD YOU'RE NOT THE TURKEY."

When I brought it home, my mom looked
at it and asked, "Did your dad get one for
himself that says, 'I AM THE TURKEY'?"

I give my dad a great big kiss hello, and
then I give mom a great big kiss goodbye.

She sort of wipes at her check.

That really hurts.

She's never wiped off my kisses before.

It's not as if I have dog germs or some-thing.

I bite my lip.

I, Amber Brown, am a little confused . . . and a lot sad . . . and then I figure it out.

Maybe she's not happy with me because I want to get my ears pierced, but I think it's because I don't think my mom likes it when my dad kisses me and then I imme-diately kiss her.

"Let's go." My dad puts his arm around me.

My mom walks us to the door and then before I leave, she leans over and gives me a great big kiss.

I give her a great big kiss back, which she doesn't wipe off her cheek.

"Make sure that she's not out too late," my mom repeats. "Tomorrow's a school day."

My dad says, "Sarah. This is my time with Amber. Joint custody, remember."

Joint custody. . . . I'm beginning to hate

those two words. I'm beginning to feel like I'm not me anymore . . . . that I'm just a part of them . . . like joint custody means each of them gets one leg, one arm . . . . or that each of them owns all of me part of the time . . . and I, Amber Brown, don't like that.

Once, when I got my hair cut too short, I told my mom how upset I was that they weren't getting along . . . . and I thought that things were going to change.

But they haven't, a lot.

My parents are so cold to each other.

It wasn't always like this.

I even remember seeing them kiss when I was younger.

Kissing.

I know that I'll have to be careful from now on.

If one parent kisses me, I can't immediately kiss the other one because it will be like they're kissing each other, sort of.

It's Divorced Parents Cooties, or something.

There should be a rulebook for kids of divorced parents with every little thing listed that we have to remember.

I, Amber Brown, think that there should also be a rulebook for parents . . . and the first rule should be that there shouldn't have to be a rulebook for their kids.

"Amber," my dad says as we get into the car, "you're with me now. Tell me why you were crying."

Chapter
Four

We just sit in Dad's car for awhile.

I, Amber Brown, have to think about what I am going to do, what I'm going to tell my Dad.

I am so angry at my mom right now.

She won't let me get my ears pierced.

She's so mean when my dad is around.

She's not acting like the Mom I've always known.

But if I say all of that to my dad, then he's going to act all proud that he's the best parent . . . and he does stuff too that drives me nuts.

I take a deep breath. "I'm just upset because Brandi called, and she and Kelly are going to the mall to get their ears pierced and I couldn't go . . ."

My dad interrupts. "Is that because you had to go with me?"

All of a sudden, a light flashes inside my head.

Well, not a light . . . . . an idea . . . . . and I'm not sure that this is a good idea . . . . but I, Amber Brown, am going to go for it. I, Amber Brown, am getting tired of the way that they are both acting. I'm tired of being in the middle . . . . and I want to do something for ME.

I sniffle and nod.

And then I sniffle again. "That's one of the reasons. But don't feel bad, Daddy, because I can get them pierced some time in the future."

I don't mention that the time in the future, according to my mom, is a little over two and a half years away.

My dad sits for a minute, thinking. "Honey, I don't want you to feel bad because we have plans and you can't do that with your friends."

"It's okay," I say, "even though they are probably on their way to the mall right now, I don't feel bad . . . not that bad anyway."

My dad turns the key in the ignition and says, "Well . . . you don't have to be upset, my wonderful daughter. I will take you to the mall . . . . and you can meet up with your friends and get your ears pierced."

"Oh, Daddy." I pat him on his hand. "Thank you soooooo much. You are so wonderful . . . . the best dad in the entire world."

"As your Aunt Pam says, wagons ho," my dad says, as he pulls the car out of the parking space.

I, Amber Brown, wonder about that.

Aunt Pam is my mom's sister, and now

that my parents are divorced, is my dad supposed to be quoting my mom's sister, his ex–sister–in–law?

I, Amber Brown, am also wondering about what I've done. . . . I haven't actually lied to my dad . . . but I haven't told him the whole truth. . . . . But I really, really want to get my ears pierced . . . . and he doesn't say no . . . . and I'm his daughter too . . . . so that means that I should be able to get at least one of my ears pierced . . . . and my mom should only get half as mad because with joint custody, they share me and they each think that they own me. . . . . So really I'll have only pierced one ear that she has custody of . . .

"Vrrrrrrrrooooooooooooooooooooom," my dad says as we drive.

That's something he used to say when I was little.

He turns his head to me and smiles.

"Vrrrrrrroooooooooooooooooooom," I say and then sing, "Off we go into the wild blue yonder."

It's part of a song that my dad used to sing to me when I was little . . . . . when he used to lift me up over his head, and I'd pretend that I was an airplane.

We both sing it together.

It's something that is ours . . . . to re-member and to do now.

We finish singing.

My dad asks, "When we get to the mall,

where should I park? Where are you all going to get your ears pierced?"

I bite my lip.

I, Amber Brown, never found out where Brandi and Kelly are going.

I close my eyes and try to figure out how to handle this.

Maybe I should tell him the truth now.

If I do, I'll probably be the only fourth-grade girl in the world who doesn't have pierced ears.

If I don't, I'll have pierced ears and one angry mom . . . and probably one angry dad . . . . but in this case, one plus one equals two . . . . two pierced ears.

I, Amber Brown, decide to go for it. "They're getting them done at Jamison's Jewelry Store . . . . but because they didn't think I could go, they may have already gotten them done. . . . If they're not there, do you think I should wait?"

I hope that he says the word that I want to hear.

Instead, as he parks the car, he says, "Amber, are they really getting their ears pierced?"

"I promise," I say and wait for him to ask what Mom thinks.

He doesn't ask.

He nods. "Then you can get yours done. I trust you."

Something tells me that I am going to feel really bad about what I am going to do, but I would feel worse if my ears don't get pierced.

I, Amber Brown, am going to get my ears pierced.

I'm very excited . . . . . and very nervous . . . and not just because my ears are going to get pierced.

Chapter Five

"Amber," my dad says as we come out of the jewelry store, "it's a shame that your friends weren't there when we got there."

I nod. "A real shame."

I don't tell my dad that I was glad that they weren't there.

They might have said something like, "Oh, it's great that your mom gave in."

Then I never would have gotten my ears pierced.

My dad looks very pleased with himself. "I'm so glad that I'm back and can be more of a part of your daily life. It was such a mistake for me to move to Paris."

"I hated it when you left, Daddy. Please don't do anything like that again," I say, touching my new gold earrings.

Just be gla...

He shakes his head. "It really was a mistake . . . . one of a long line of them I made at that time."

"What do you mean?" I ask.

He shakes his head again and then changes the subject. "For Christmas, would you like me to get you some more earrings for when you can take those out, when the holes are all better?"

I nod.

Something tells me that my mom is not going to be buying me earrings for Christmas.

Mom . . . . I wonder what she's going to do.

She's definitely not going to be a happy camper.

But Dad said I could get it done.

I didn't even have to ask him.

He just said I could.

Something tells me that this is the worst thing that I, Amber Brown, have ever done in my whole entire life.

But they deserve it, treating me like I have no right to do what I want . . . it's all got to be what they want and need . . . .

43

joint custody. . . . Well, I have ear custody . . . and I've just done what I want and need.

I feel really scared because my dad feels so good about what he's done, and I know that he's not going to feel so good when my mom finds out.

And I, Amber Brown, am not so sure that I feel good about what I've just done.

I'm getting a headache, and I don't think it's from the ear piercing.

My dad says, "Amber, I have a surprise for you."

"What?" I ask.

"If I tell you, it won't be a surprise. Hurry up. We have to be somewhere by six o'clock."

As we leave the mall, my stomach starts to growl and I say, "Dad, where are we going for dinner tonight? Fast food? Or slow food?"

Slow food is what my dad and I call going to a regular restaurant.

Since my dad has moved back, we eat out all of the time.

That's because he's staying with his friends the Donaldsons until he finds an apartment, but we don't go there to eat because he says that he doesn't want to be an "inconvenience."

"Where we are eating is part of the surprise," he says.

Oh no . . . a food surprise . . . the last time he said that, he took me to a Japanese restaurant and we ate sushi. Raw fish. At first, I felt like I was eating something that had once been a pet in a fishbowl, but then I got used to some of it and actually liked some of it . . . . except for something called uni that made me want to puke. And the octopus and the squid were gross, very gross . . . and not just because it felt like they belonged in *The Little Mermaid* movie.

So when my dad says "food surprise," I,

Amber Brown, get a little nervous.

I, Amber Brown, am also hungry.

And I am also curious.

I touch my new earrings and wish that my father would tell me what's going on.

I wish that my father would feed me.

At home, it's so easy.

I get hungry . . . . . I go into the kitchen and get something.

With my dad, it's different.

We have to go somewhere to get something unless it's just a snack that we can eat in his car.

It's kind of weird.

We've left the mall, and we're not heading to any place where I know that there is a restaurant.

We're going down a regular street, not far from my street.

It's not even the street where the Donaldsons live.

My dad parks in front of a house.

"We're home," he says.

I, Amber Brown, am not only very hungry.

I am very confused.

Chapter
Six

"Home sweet home," my father says.

I look at him.

Then I try to look at the house.

It's dark outside, but I can see that it's a real house.

There are lights on upstairs.

I look at my father. "Whose home sweet home?"

My dad says, "Ours . . . . well, ours and the Marshall family. I decided not to rent an apartment in an apartment building . . . and I didn't want to rent a whole big house. So, when a buddy of mine at work mentioned that his tenant had moved out, I asked to see the place. I liked what I saw and rented it yesterday. Actually, there are two places to live in the house. We've got the basement and first floor. The Marshalls live on the top two floors. Come on. Let's go in. I want you to see it. And then we're going to have dinner with Steve and his kids."

I continue to sit in the car.

My dad comes over to my door, opens it and pretends to be the chauffeur.

I continue to sit in the car.

"Amber, honey. Get out. They're all waiting to have dinner with us," he says.

I continue to sit in the car and stare out the front window.

I don't even look at him.

I have so many feelings inside, I feel like I'm going to explode.

I'm confused . . . . . upset . . . . angry . . . . jealous . . . . . sad . . . . and I don't know what to say.

It serves him right that I tricked him into helping me get my ears pierced.

I continue to sit in the car, looking out the window, and the tears start to come out of my eyes and down my face.

I really don't want to cry.

"Amber." He kneels down by the open car door. "Come on. It's cold out here . . . . and I don't understand what's the matter. I don't have a clue."

That's my dad . . . Clueless . . . Clueless Dad . . . . Clueless Dad Brown.

I, Amber Brown, am so angry at him.

"Amber," he says again. "Look at me. Tell me what's wrong. Why are you crying? I really hate it when you cry."

I look at him, but don't say anything for a minute.

He looks back. "Amber. Please. I want this to be a wonderful time. It's my new home . . . . our new home. . . . You're really going to love it."

My nose starts to run, just a little.

I sniffle.

I sniffle again and then I say, "You promised."

"I promised?" he asks.

"You promised that I would go with you to help you pick out the apartment that you were going to rent . . . that I would be part of the deciding . . . . and now you've gone and decided without me."

He leans against the car . . . . . . and says nothing.

I continue. "And now I find out that it's a HOUSE with other people living in it. Steve and his kids . . . is there a Mrs. Steve?. . . . What if I don't like these kids? What if they don't like me?"

"They'll love you, honey. Everyone loves you," my father says.

"Not everyone," I say, thinking of one of the kids in my class who I can't get along with. "Please don't tell me that one of the kids is Hannah Burton."

"No Hannah Burton in the house." My father shakes his head. "Honey, there's no one from your class in the house. Two of them go to your school. One of them goes to high school. Their last name is Marshall. Steve Marshall and his kids. . . . There's Polly, Dylan, and Savannah. Steve and his wife are separated . . . and the kids live with their father."

Savannah. I think I know her.

She's a third grader, in Mr. Cohen's class.

And I think I know who Dylan is.

He's one of the sixth graders . . . one of those kids who thinks that they own the whole school because they are the oldest kids there.

He once called me "Squirt."

I don't know Polly.

And I don't want to leave the car.

And there's something else that is bothering me . . . bothering me big time.

I want my dad to say that he's sorry that he broke a promise to me.

"Honey," my Dad says. "It'll be just fine. I promise."

How can I trust him?

"Mr. Brown. Amber," someone yells out. I look over to see Savannah Marshall coming toward us.

It would serve my dad right if I asked to go home right now . . . back to my mom's and my home, where I can depend on certain things . . . where I'm used to certain things.

But with my newly pierced ears, I'm not sure that I want to go home yet.

I look over at my dad's sad face and then at Savannah's smiling face.

My stomach starts to growl.

I sniffle again.

I can't let a third grader see me cry.

I, Amber Brown, have to make a decision.

And I'm not sure what it is.

Chapter Seven

Savannah looks in the car and stares at me.

Then she looks at my father.

Then she looks at me again. "Are you okay?"

I sniffle.

I'm glad that it's getting dark so that she can't see how red and puffy my eyes are and that my face looks splotchy.

Inside my brain, I try to convince my eyes not to be all red and puffy and for my face to look non-splotchy.

Just in case that doesn't work, I say, "Allergies. I have allergies."

"To what?" She looks concerned.

I want to say "To Clueless Dads," but instead I say, "To lots of things. . . . But don't worry. I'll be okay."

My dad stands up and holds out his hand to help me get out of the car.

I think about it for a minute and make my decision.

"No thanks," I say. "I can do it myself."

My dad puts his hand back down.

I get out of the car.

I, Amber Brown, will go inside.

He's already rented it.

There's nothing I can do about that.

If I hate it, I'll never come back again.

Savannah smiles at me, and together we start walking to the house.

I am not paying any attention to my father who is walking with us.

"You're in Mr. Cohen's class," I sort of say, sort of ask.

She nods and keeps smiling.

"Lucky," I say. "He's a great teacher."

"I know," Savannah says.

My dad is walking next to me, but I'm not even looking at him, not even talking to him.

We get to the front door and go in.

There are steps straight ahead.

To the left of the steps farther back, there's a door.

My dad touches my shoulder. "Amber,

honey . . . that's where we are going to live."

I turn to Savannah and say, "I already live on Chestnut Street."

She says, "This is Elm Street . . . . so you are going to live in two places that are named after trees."

I, Amber Brown, will have two houses . . . . . on two streets named after trees.

I wonder if that means that I will be living in treehouses.

That makes me smile until I start to think about how much my life is changing.

All of a sudden, this seems very real to me.

I, Amber Brown, will finally have two houses . . . . . one where I live with my mom . . . . one where I live with my dad . . . joint custody.

It's weird.

When my dad had an apartment in our town for a short time after he and Mom broke up and then he moved to Paris, I always felt like I was just visiting there.

Now he expects me to have a home with him, not just at my mom's and my place.

Part of me likes the idea.

Part of me is not so sure.

"Want me to show this place to you?" Savannah says. "I can pretend that I'm the real estate lady, and you can be the customer."

For a minute, I think about how much fun it would be to pretend.

I, Amber Brown, love to pretend.

But this time it isn't pretend.

It's for real.

My dad says, "Savannah, thank you. But I really want to show the place to Amber myself. And I would like a few minutes alone to speak with her. So would you please go upstairs now and tell your dad that we'll be up for dinner in about ten or fifteen minutes?"

Savannah looks disappointed.

I'm a little disappointed too.

It's always fun to find other people who like to play, even if they are a little younger.

Savannah goes upstairs.

I look at my dad, not smiling . . . . waiting for him to say something.

He does. "Amber. I'm sorry."

Finally.

I continue to look at him.

He continues. "I should have let you see this first. I'm sorry that I broke my promise. It just seemed like such a good idea. It's a great place . . . and Steve has become a friend, and he has nice kids. They are a good family . . . and sometimes . . . sometimes, Amber, I feel very lonely. I've just gotten back from Paris. You're with your mom most of the time. I work all day, stay late at the office because I don't want to get in the Donaldsons' way. I suppose that I should have gotten a hotel room until I found a place, but that felt really lonely."

Twice my dad has said that he's lonely.
I, Amber Brown, feel sad for him.
He's my dad.
I don't want him to feel lonely.
I give him a big hug.
He hugs me back.
Then he gives me a kiss on the forehead.
"I love you so much."

"Me too," I say.
"Am I forgiven?" he asks.
I nod.
I hope that he's going to forgive me for
what I've done, getting my ears pierced.

Then I think of the other promise that he made that I really hope that he has not broken.

"Dad," I say, "it's okay as long as I still get to help pick out the furniture."

"It's a deal." He crosses his heart.

Now I, Amber Brown, am ready to see the house.

Chapter Eight

"The doorway to our home," my dad says, opening it. "There's also an entrance to our apartment from the back. This room will be the living room."

It's one big empty room.

"It will also be the dining area." He points to one side of the room, "if we don't feel like eating in the kitchen."

I nod.

There's not much to say.

It's one big empty room.

"Honey, look." My Dad walks over to the

windows at the back of the room. "Doesn't this look great?"

I join him and look out the window.

There's a really nice backyard, with trees and swings and a treehouse . . . there really is a treehouse on Elm Street.

"We can use the backyard and share it with the Marshalls," he says.

I, Amber Brown, think about how Savannah and I can play in the treehouse . . . and how my friends, Brandi and Kelly, can come over and play in it too.

I can't wait to write to Justin and tell him that he's not the only one with a treehouse, that I now have one too.

Then I remember. . . . I'm not sure yet that this is going to be one of my houses.

My dad puts his arm around my shoulder and says, "Let's look at the rest of this place."

The kitchen.

It's a kitchen. . . . Since I'm not much of a cook, kitchens aren't that important to me . . . . except as a place to eat and talk.

"I hope that you don't mind," my dad says. "I went out and bought some pots and pans . . . dishes, silverware, supplies."

I go over to the refrigerator and look inside. "And some food."

He nods. "I didn't think you would mind if I did that without you."

I shake my head. "That's fine."

I pick up the peanut butter jar. "Dad. This

is creamy peanut butter. I, Amber Brown, like chunky peanut butter."

He grins. "Then . . . . . I, Philip Brown, will get chunky peanut butter for my daughter, Amber Brown . . . . or is your name now I, Amber Brown????"

I giggle.

He says, "Well, . . . I, Amber Brown . . . . why do you like referring to yourself that way?"

I, Amber Brown, think about it.

I answer: "It makes me strong to say my name that way. Like I belong to myself . . . and am not just Amber Brown, your daughter, mom's daughter, Mrs. Holt's student. . . . I am I, AMBER BROWN. . . . You don't have to call me that . . . I just have to know that's who I am . . . and I want other people to know that's who I am."

He whistles. "For someone who is only nine, you are very sure of that."

I nod.

I am.

Divorce can do that to a kid.

Just living can do that to a kid.

I look around the room. "Okay . . . so now, where's my bedroom? If I decide to live here part time, where will I sleep? Do I, Amber Brown, have a room?"

"Yes. You, Amber Brown, do have a room. It's downstairs . . . but first I want to show you this floor."

There's not much left to show . . . a bathroom . . . . and a room with a sleeping bag in it.

"This is my bedroom," he says. "Tomorrow, I'm going to Ikea to buy some furniture. We'll talk to your mom about your taking the day off from school. It'll be so much fun. . . . . . . A Dad and Daughter Shop Day . . . . and it's important that we go tomorrow. The timing is very important. If we order the furniture tomorrow, it can be delivered in a few days and then a company can come over and assemble it all in one day. That way the house will be ready by Christmas . . . . our almost-instant home. I have the catalog for you to look at, to make some preliminary decisions and then we'll make the final ones at the store."

No school . . . . shopping with my dad . . . . I, Amber Brown, will like that.

He hands me a catalog.

Before I can look at it, he says, "Let me show you the downstairs. That's where your room is."

Great, I think. Downstairs in my house with Mom is the basement where we keep the washer and dryer. It's not really finished, and it's a little creepy, with cobwebs.

So in this house, he's putting me down in the basement to live like some creature in a horror book, where the monster lives in the dungeon.

He'll probably throw down scraps of bread with chunky peanut butter for me to live on.

I follow him downstairs.

This basement looks terrific.

"This will be the recreation room. We'll put the TV in here . . . . and the computer . . . and a place to do jigsaw puzzles. . . . Remember when you were little . . . how we always used to do them," my dad says.

I remember.

I was a little kid then.

We used to do Sesame Street puzzles, and ones with Mickey Mouse and Goofy.

I hope that my dad doesn't want to do those anymore.

I'm too old to do a Goofy puzzle or goofy puzzles.

I gave all my old puzzles away a long time ago to Justin's little brother, Danny.

My dad holds up a box. "I've already bought one. We can work on it every time you come to visit."

I make a face and think. . . . . Please not a little kid puzzle.

I know that my dad's been away for awhile, but he can't think that I'm still that little.

I walk over to look at the puzzle, hoping that he didn't buy a Barney puzzle. I, Amber Brown, have never liked that purple dinosaur, even though purple is my favorite color.

"See." My dad looks so proud of himself.

I see.

I smile.

It's a terrific 3-D puzzle.

It looks like a big clock, with stars and moons and rainbows on it . . . and it's not only a puzzle . . . . it IS a real clock, one that has stuff in the box that will make the clock run. It's soooooooo fun!

"When we finish it, we can hang it on the wall." My dad points to a spot. "Right here . . . . or is there some other place that you think it should go?"

I smile again. "It'll be perfect there."

He looks very happy. "Now for your room."

He walks to the back and opens a door. "Ta dum."

It's the bathroom.

"My room?" I ask. "Am I supposed to sleep in the tub?"

"Oops," he says. "Wrong door. I'm still not sure of where everything is. This all happened so quickly."

He goes over to the next door. "Ta dum."

I look inside.

It's a really big room . . . . about twice the size of my bedroom at my mom's. . . . . And there's a loft bed already in it.

A loft bed is just so great. It's like a tree-house in your own room . . . . like a giant bunk bed with no lower bunk.

I rush inside and look up at the loft bed.

"This was here already," Dad says. "Do you want this or a regular bed?"

I put my foot up on the first rung of the ladder by the side of the loft bed. "Are you kidding? I want this. It's sooooooooooooo great."

Very quickly, I go up the ladder.

There's enough room up here for a double mattress . . . . for a whole lot of stuffed animals . . . and for me.

The ceiling is so high that I can sit up straight on the bed and still have space left over.

My father climbs up the ladder, sits down and hits his head on the ceiling.

I look up at the ceiling over the loft bed area. . . . There are fluorescent stars and moons and planets on it.

I just know that they are going to glow in the dark.

"I love this," I say.

"Then we'll live here," my dad says. "That's okay with you . . . . yes??"

I nod. "When I'm staying with you, this is great. But don't forget. . . . I'm still living with Mom too."

He nods, and then we hug each other.

"What," I ask "would you have done if I had said no?"

He shakes his head. "I don't know. I honestly don't know. I'm just glad that you didn't say no."

I look at him. "Dad. Promise me that from now on when you make a promise, you will keep it."

He nods. "I'll do my best."

That makes me a little nervous.

I really wish that he had just said, "Yes. I promise."

Saying "I'll do my best" leaves him a lot of chances to make more mistakes.

I'm not sure that I like that in a parent.

But I think about what he's done. . . . He's found a place that's nice, with a room for me that I love. . . . And it was really nice of him to remember that we used to put puzzles together. . . . . And we're going to be able to shop together for things for the house.

I, Amber Brown, am going to give this a chance.

I only hope that it turns out all right.

Chapter Nine

"Now for something else that is really exciting," my dad says, taking me to the third floor. "You're going to meet the Marshalls."

He knocks at the door.

In about a second and a half, the door is opened.

Savannah is jumping up and down. "Finally."

Behind her is Dylan, who is standing there with a french fry up his nose.

Behind Dylan is a grown-up who, dad-like, takes the french fry out of Dylan's nose and then comes up to me.

"Welcome, Amber." He reaches out to shake my hand. "I'm Steve Marshall."

First, I make sure that he's not using the hand that has the french fry in it.

He's not . . . . so I shake his hand.

"Welcome, Amber." A teenage girl comes up to me. "Hi, I'm Polly."

She's wearing black tights and a very large black T-shirt and lots of jewelry.

Behind her, someone yells, "SUR-PRISE!"

It's Brenda, my Ambersitter, the best sitter in the whole wide world . . . if you don't count the fact that she is also one of the world's worst cooks.

For other people, Brenda just baby-sits. For me she Ambersits.

Today Brenda's hair is spiky and pink and glitters with orange and purple.

She definitely has gone crazy with cans of glitter spray.

We rush up to each other. "What are you doing here?" I give her a hug.

"Polly is my best friend." She hugs back.

Polly. She's talked about Polly. I just didn't put it all together that Polly Marshall is the Polly who is Brenda's best friend. In fact, this whole thing is happening so quickly that I'm having trouble putting lots of stuff together.

She looks at me.

Then she looks at me again.

"Amber. When did you get your ears pierced?" she asks.

I almost forgot. "Today."

She looks at me and then she looks at my dad, who is talking to Mr. Marshall.

Brenda leans over and whispers, "Does your mom know about this? Did you get her permission?"

Biting my lip, I shake my head no.

Brenda kind of makes a gulping sound and softly says, "Wow."

"Okay," Mr. Marshall says, "you've already met Savannah . . . and this is my son, Dylan . . . . who seems to think it's funny to adorn himself with french fries."

I smile at Savannah . . . and look at Dylan, who now has french fries in his ears.

His father takes them out of Dylan's ears. "If you do that one more time, I'm going to make you eat the french fries that you have stuck in your ears and nose. Now stop doing that."

Dylan smiles. "No nose. No ears."

"And not any other parts of your body either," his dad says.

"Darn," Dylan says.

I, Amber Brown, don't want to think about where else Dylan was thinking of sticking those french fries.

"Okay, everyone," Mr. Marshall says, "it's time to eat. Amber, I hope that you like hot dogs and beans and hamburgers."

"Yum," I say.

It's kind of a party, only it's one where I only know three people well . . . . my dad and Brenda and me.

The table is already set.

I am very hungry.

We all sit down and eat.

I prepare one of my favorite meals . . . . hot dog in a roll with beans on top of that, and then mustard and ketchup on top of that, and potato chips with ridges on top of that.

Then I put some french fries on the side. Yum.

The Marshalls are definitely not a quiet family.

I, Amber Brown, am used to meals with just my mom . . . . or now, sometimes with my mom and Max.

They are definitely not this noisy.

Here, everyone is joking around, teasing each other.

At my house, we joke and tease too, but it's not this loud.

One of the reasons that it is so noisy is that Dylan is having races with hot dogs in hot dog rolls. "Okay, sports fans . . . . which one will be the winner??? Will it be the one wearing the coat of yellow (the mustard) or will it be the one wearing the red coat. (No, he's not British . . . he's wearing catsup.) It's the yellow one in the lead. . . . . But can he cut the mustard?? Wow!!! Look!!! The one in red is not far behind . . . . and he's get-

ting closer .... closer .... now he's pulling
in front. Boy, does that hot dog know how
to catsup."

Dylan keeps laughing at his own jokes.

His dad laughs at them too.

My mom would never let Dylan do that
at the table.

Thinking that makes me think about what
else my mom would not allow. . . . .
And I've just done it.

I get very nervous if I think about what's

going to happen when my mom finds out.

I look back at Dylan.

He's put more french fries up his nose, crossed his eyes at me and opened his mouth, which is filled with chewed up hamburger.

Something tells me that he and Justin would really have gotten along.

If Dylan thinks he's going to gross me out by doing things like that, he's not. When we were little, Justin and I used to put cheerios up our noses . . . and sometimes Justin would even add milk to his. So, if Dylan thinks that he's going to gross me out, I'm going to have to tell him about the chewing gum ball that Justin and I once made.

So what Dylan is doing with his french fries is just small potatoes to me.

His dad finally makes him stop, but I bet that Dylan is not going to stay stopped for long.

Brenda sits next to me.

That makes me feel good.

When I woke up today, I had one kind of life . . . . and now, BAM, without any warning, I've got a different kind of life . . . so it's good that Brenda is here. I know her. She doesn't change . . . . except for her hair color . . . and that's not such a big deal.

She's so excited that my dad is renting the downstairs. "And, Amber, sometimes when your dad goes out at night, I can Ambersit for you here, and we can all hang out and have a good time."

I look at my dad, who nods.

I wonder where he's going to be going out when I come here . . . and who he is going to be going out with.

Brenda continues. "And if you want and if there is time, we can go through the Ikea catalog and help you pick out things for your room . . . so that when you go shopping, you'll already have an idea of what you want."

Everything is happening so quickly.

I ask, "Brenda, how long have you known about this?"

She says, "Two days. Polly called me when your dad decided to rent the place . . . . and then yesterday after your dad went shopping, he came over here and Polly and I were doing our science project. We all started talking. We offered to help you with your room if you want."

I nod.

Dylan starts pretending that he's going to

squirt catsup at Savannah, who starts yelling.

While Mr. Marshall gives Dylan one more chance before he has to leave the table, Brenda leans over to me and whispers, "I couldn't tell you when I found out. They made me promise. Your dad wanted to be the one to tell you."

I nod and bite my lip.

"Are you okay with all of this?" she whispers.

I shrug. "I think so. I don't know."

My dad is looking over at us, and I just know that he is trying to listen so I just sit there.

Brenda smiles at me. "Amber. It's going to be so much fun. Don't worry. You're really lucky. . . . You have a great home with your mom, and now you're going to have a great home with your dad."

I, Amber Brown, hope that's true.

My father leans over and says, "Amber. Don't forget what they said at the jewelry

86

store. You've got to put some of that ointment on your ears so that they don't get infected."

Brenda says, "I'll help her with that, Mr. Brown. If you will all excuse us for a few minutes, I'll put the ointment on so that we don't forget."

Once Brenda and I go into the bathroom so that I can privately put the ointment on my earlobes, she says, "Amber, I thought your mom told you that you couldn't have your ears pierced until you were twelve."

I try my reasoning out on her. "But my dad said that it was okay . . . and anyway it's my body, not anyone else's."

She shakes her head. "No go."

"But you have a lot of holes on your ears," I say.

"I also have a mother who gave me permission. . . . She has said that I am not to get my tongue pierced, though . . . . but I don't want to do that anyway."

"Ugh," I say.

My earlobes hurt enough.

I, Amber Brown, can not imagine what it would be like to have a pierced tongue . . . . and I'm not going to find out.

That's not something that my mother will even have to tell me not to do.

"Amber Brown," Brenda the Ambersitter says, "I don't want to be around when you have to tell your mother that you've gotten your ears pierced."

Actually, I, Amber Brown, don't want to be around then either.

Chapter
Ten

"This has been a great day," my dad says, as we park in a space in front of Mom's and my house.

"Yes," I say, touching my ears.

Part of me wishes that I hadn't gotten them pierced today because I know that this day is not going to stay a great day.

"Wait 'til your mom sees your ears." My dad smiles at me.

"Wait 'til my mom sees my ears," I say, in a very quiet voice.

"Dad," I say. "Let's just sit out in the car

for a few minutes. I want to spend a little more time with you."

My dad grins.

He is soooooooooo happy that I want to spend more time with him.

And I do . . . . . and this would all be soooooo much easier if I didn't have to deal with my pierced ears and my mother.

I, Amber Brown, have wanted pierced ears for a long time and always have imagined what a happy day it would be when I finally got them.

My dad talks to me about how much fun it will be to furniture shop, how he wants to do it tomorrow. "I hope that your mother says that it's okay for you to take the day off from school. I really want to have the furniture all done by Christmas. Our house will feel so much more like a home if it is all filled with furniture."

I just nod.

My dad looks at his watch. "Honey, let's

go in now. I promised your mom that we would be back early so that you could check your homework. We don't want to do anything that will make her angry."

Too late for that, I think.

We get out of the car and walk to the door.

My dad rings the bell.

"We can just go in," I say.

My dad shakes his head. "You can just go in. . . . I can't. This is your mom's and your house . . . and I don't live here anymore, so I ring the bell."

There's so much to figure out, to work out.

My dad is trying very hard to do it all right.

I, Amber Brown, am feeling guilty for making it not all right.

"Dad," I say. "I can go in by myself. You can call Mom later."

I figure that way she'll get angry at me

first and then calm down a little by the time she talks to him.

The door opens.

It's too late.

"Sarah. Would you mind if I came in? There's something that I would like to ask you."

"Okay," she says. "Come in."

She walks into the living room, and we all sit down.

I jump up again. "I'll go upstairs and check over my homework."

"Good idea," my mom says.

I rush to go out the door and up to my room.

"Amber. Wait," my dad calls out. "Before you go, show your mom what we had done today."

I just stand there.

I look at my dad.

I look at my mom.

I cover my ears.

"Amber," my mother says softly, "show me what you did today."

"Mom," I say.

"Amber," she says.

"Amber," my dad says. "What's going on? Show your mom your new earrings."

My mom jumps up, comes over to where I am standing and says, "Amber. Take your hands away from your ears . . . . and let me see what you have done."

I take my hands away from my ears.

She looks at my newly pierced ears.

"How could you???" she yells. "I told you that you would have to wait until you are twelve."

I start to cry.

She turns to my dad and yells. "And how dare you?? How dare you go against something that I have made a rule about!"

My dad says, "But I didn't know."

He looks at me.

He looks angry and sad and hurt.

"Sarah," he says. "I had no idea."

"I bet you didn't," she says, angrily.

"I didn't." Now my dad sounds angry. "Do you think that I would have done this if I knew that you had said no? We would have talked about it first if I had any idea."

"Well, you should have checked with me," she says.

"You're not the only rule maker in this family." My dad folds his arms in front of him.

"And you are not a part of this family." My mother makes a terrible face at him.

I, Amber Brown, feel sick to my stomach.

This was such a great day until now.

And now the ungreat part is just starting.

"I may not be a part of your family . . . BUT I am still a part of Amber's family . . . and I have some rights here," my dad says. "She's my daughter too."

"And where have you been when I've had to make all the decisions? You've been in Paris . . . . and now you waltz back here and expect to be able to do just what you want . . . when you want to. Philip. . . ." My mom takes a deep breath and tries to calm down. "How could you do something like this? After I told Amber today that she would have to wait."

"I told you . . . . . . I didn't know that," he says, looking at me.

My stomach is hurting a lot, and I don't think it's because of my hot dog meal.

I look at my dad.

I look at my mom.

I start to yell. "I'm sick of this. You each

think you own me. Daddy, you come back
from Paris and now there's all this fighting
about what I can do and when. Mom says
one thing. You say the other. I feel like I
have no say. I don't even know who I, Amber
Brown, am anymore. . . . I feel like it's all
up to each of you . . . and that sometimes
it's not even about me . . . . it's just another
way for you two to fight."

I stamp my foot.

I've never acted like this.

I am so mad that I stamp my foot again. "There . . . . that's one stamp for each of you . . . so that neither of you feel left out . . . so that neither of you feel like I'm not angry at both of you."

"Amber," my dad says. "I don't get it. We've had a great time today . . . and it's not my fault that you didn't tell me that your mom said you shouldn't get your ears pierced. If anyone here should be angry . . . it should be me . . . . and your mother. You haven't been fair to either of us."

I stamp my feet again. "Oh, okay . . . . . so NOW I see. . . . . You can both be angry but I can't . . . . it's the two of you . . . . not me. Well, I'm sick of it."

I start to cry again.

My mom looks at me. I want her to come over and hug me.

But she doesn't.

I really want my mom to hug me.

But she doesn't.

And my dad isn't hugging me either.

I, Amber Brown, feel just awful.

My mom says, "Amber. I want you to go upstairs for now, to your room. I want you to think about what you've done. And while you are doing that, your father and I are going to talk. We'll call you down after we've talked. Now go to your room right now."

"But," I start.

"Right now," she says, folding her arms in front of her.

I go to my room right now.

And I don't think I ever want to leave it again.

Chapter
Eleven

I can't even look at my spelling list.

I can't even think about checking my homework.

My parents are downstairs.

I hope that they don't yell at each other.

I hope that they don't do something awful.

I hope that they don't yell at me.

I hope that this all turns out okay.

I hope that they still love me.

I pick up a mirror and look at my stupid earrings.

Why did I do something so dumb?

Why?

I think about the reasons why.

I wanted pierced ears.

I like jewelry.

All of my friends were getting their ears pierced, and I would be the only doofus without pierced ears.

Well . . . . I know not the *only* one . . . . but all my good friends (except Justin).

My mom is angry at my dad.

My dad is angry at my mom.

They are both angry at me.

I look at the earrings in the mirror.

They are pretty little gold balls . . . . just the kind that I always wanted as my starter set.

Now they'll probably tarnish, turn black, infect my earlobes, and then an infection will spread throughout my entire body.

And then I'll die . . . . and my parents will be so sorry.

I bite my lip.

Maybe they won't be so sorry.

If I'm not around, they will never have to see each other again.

I know that they'd both like that.

Well, my mom would like that.

Sometimes I think my dad still cares about my mom and wishes that they hadn't broken up . . . but now they are fighting again so who knows?

If I'm not around, my mom and Max can get married and start all over again . . . . have other kids, ones who don't want their ears pierced.

If I'm not around, my dad can live anywhere in the world that he wants to live . . . . so he won't have to stay in a place just to have joint custody.

Maybe they'll have joint custody of my grave.

I'll write out a will and leave each of them one of my earrings.

I get a note pad and pen and lie down on my bed.

My stuffed toy gorilla is sitting next to
me.

"What should I leave to you?" I ask him.

He says nothing.

He is really a stuffed animal so I realize
that I can't leave him anything, I will have
to leave him to someone.

Brandi will get him . . . . and I'll leave
the dolphin, Sushi, to Kelly.

Justin will regain custody of our chewing gum ball.

I hope that every once in a while, he will
chew a piece of gum, add it to the ball, and
think of me.

"Amber," my mother says, and then knocks on my door.

"Come in," I say.

She walks in the door and looks at me. "I'm glad to see that you are doing your homework."

"I'm writing my will," I say.

She looks surprised, and then she starts to smile.

I can tell that she is trying not to laugh.

I don't think it's funny, my writing my will.

"You can finish that after you come downstairs and talk with me and your father," she says.

I get up off my bed.

I just want my mom to hug me, and she isn't doing that.

We go downstairs.

My parents have been drinking coffee.

They seem very calm.

I sit down.

They both look at me.

For a minute, none of us say anything.

They both keep looking at me.

My mom speaks first. "Amber. Do you know what you have done that is wrong?"

I sigh.

I wish that they would tell me what I did rather than making me guess . . . . or tell them.

"Yes," I say. "I asked your permission to do something and you said no . . . and then I did it anyway."

She nods. "And?"

"And I'm sorry." I say.

"That's good," she says. "And . . . ."

Now, I, Amber Brown, am lost.

I've told her what I did.

I said I was sorry.

"And . . . ." both of my parents say at the same time.

Usually when two people say the same

thing at the same time, I yell "pinkies" and the two people have to link pinkies.

This time I don't think it is a good time.

Probably if I yelled "Thumbs down" that would be something that they would do . . . . to me.

"And . . . ." I say, and then pause. "You've got to help me with this, please."

My mom shakes her head but my dad

speaks. "And you got me involved in it. You never told me that your mom said no."

"But I didn't lie," I say.

"But you didn't tell the truth," my mom says.

My dad nods.

This is soooooooooooo hard.

I wish that there was something that I could do.

All of this talking is making me very nervous.

I just want to get to the end of this conversation to find out what is going to happen to me, to my earrings, to my going shopping, to their ever loving me again.

We talk . . . . . about what I did . . . . . how from now on, my mom and dad are going to talk things out, let each other know what's happening, what they feel . . . . they also say that they will talk to me about what I feel . . . . . and that there will be times of disagreement, but we'll all try to work it out.

I have to promise not to "play one parent against the other."

"Can I go shopping with Dad tomorrow?" I ask.

"No," they both say at exactly the same time.

It's another "link pinkies" moment . . . . only I wish that they had both said yes.

I've wanted my parents to agree on stuff for a long time.

Now I'm not so sure that I like it.

My mom says, "Your father has explained to me why it is so important to get the furniture now. So after we're done talking about all of this, you and your father will be able to look at the catalogs and pick things out that way. But you can NOT take the day off."

My dad nods.

"So that's my punishment?" I ask.

"Part of it . . . although even if you weren't being punished, I don't think that I would have allowed you to miss school. . . . I don't think Mrs. Holt would have given permission. As for the rest of your punishment, we're still working that out . . . . we're not totally sure of what we are going to do, what you will have to do."

"May I keep the earrings?" I ask.

My mom sighs. "I have to think about that. There are so many choices. At the moment I am thinking that you will have to take them out tonight and let the holes close up, but I'm not sure."

At the moment, I, Amber Brown, am thinking that I don't like what my mom is thinking.

I am hoping that I can get her to change her mind.

I look over at my dad and make a kind of begging face.

He shakes his head. "This is a decision that your mother and I have to make together."

He looks at my mom and frowns. "And it's one that we haven't been able to reach agreement on."

She looks at him and frowns back.

I have one very annoyed mom, and I don't think that I'm the only one that she is annoyed with.

I think that my dad is also annoyed.

. . . . And I don't think that this is just about me.

I'm afraid that my parents are going to start fighting with each other.

The doorbell rings.

Saved by the bell.

Chapter
Twelve

This has turned into the longest day of my life.

Most days, there's just normal every day things happening.

Today, more things have happened than usually happens in a week: wake up . . . . . make presents . . . . uncrazyglue myself . . . . . go out with my dad, get my ears pierced, see my new house and meet a whole bunch of new people who are now going to be part of my life . . . . and then it's back home with mom finding out about my ears . . . . going to my room . . . . making a will . . . then there's this big scene with my parents . . . . and now the doorbell rings.

I, Amber Brown, am not sure that more can happen on this day.

I rush to the door.

"I'm home," the voice says.

It's Max.

This is not really his home.

He doesn't stay here . . . but he likes to say that to practice for when he and Mom will be married and he will be living here.

I hope that my dad doesn't hear Max say, "I'm home."

I open the door.

He's carrying a huge box of things for our bowling team's Christmas party. There is a Pinster Piñata that I helped him make when Mom and I went over to his house one day. There is a battery-run bowling Santa . . . and the pins are his elves. I painted the pins to look like elves. And there are candies and cookies and little awards for each person on the team.

Max is the best coach in the world.

"So what happened on this day of December 12?" Max asks.

I remember what I read this morning. "On this day in 1901, some guy named Macaroni sent the first radio signal across the Atlantic Ocean. It went from Cornwall, England, to Newfoundland, Canada."

Max smiles. "Marconi. Not Macaroni. . . . . Unless he had a pasta life."

Max laughs at his own joke, which I, Amber Brown, don't get.

"Where's our Sarah?" he asks.

"They went into the kitchen," I say. "She and Dad are talking."

He walks into the kitchen.

When Mom sees Max, she jumps up and gives him a kiss.

Then Max says hello to my dad.

My dad says hello back.

Neither of them is smiling.

I take a deep breath and wonder what's going to happen next.

Mom says, "Honey."

All three of us say "Yes."

My dad, Max, and me.

"Max." My mom kisses his cheek. "Amber and Philip are going to be in the kitchen for awhile, picking out some things for Philip's new house."

Max nods.

Mom continues. "So let's go into the living room and talk about the team's Christmas party. Let's let Philip and Amber do their selecting."

"Okay." Max goes over to the refrigerator, opens the door, and pulls out a can of root beer for himself and a can of seltzer for my mom. "Can I interest either of you in something to drink?"

My dad shakes his head no.

I ask for and get some orange juice.

My dad watches as they leave the room.

Then he opens the catalog and says, "On your mark . . . . . . get set . . . . . . shop. We have a house that we want to turn into a home."

And we shop.

Chapter Thirteen

"*Barukh atah Adonai, Eloheynu melekh ha-olam, asher kid'shanu be-mitzvotav ve-tzivanu le-hadlik ner shel Hanukkah.*" Max recites the blessing in Hebrew as he lights the candles on the menorah.

I, Amber Brown, read the English translation. "Praised are You, O Lord, Our God, King of the Universe, who sanctified us with His commandments and commanded us to kindle the Hanukkah lights."

"It's time to play with the dreidel," Max says.

Mom, Max, and I spin the dreidel and I, Amber Brown, win a lot of candy money.

Then we give each other presents.

I, Amber Brown, tell Max to open his first even though I really want to open mine first. I really want him to like his present.

Actually, I really love opening presents so Max lets me unwrap his, and then he looks at the bowling salt and pepper shakers.

"Just what I needed!" He gives me a hug.

"Even though you already have salt and pepper shakers at your house?" I ask.

He nods. "I really need these. My house has been wanting things that are made for me by a child whom I love."

"And who loves you," I say softly.

We give each other a hug.

I look over at my mom.

She's starting to cry, just a little.

But she's smiling a lot.

"Are you crying because you know that in about six months these salt and pepper shakers will be living with us? I know that they are not your favorite items," I tease her.

She wipes at her tears and keeps on smiling. "No. I'm just happy. You know that."

"Open your present." I hand it to her. "It's from Max and me."

She starts to unwrap the present and then hands it to me. "You can unwrap it if you want."

I want.

I do love unwrapping presents, even if they are not for me, even if I am giving them to the other person and know exactly what's in it.

I hand it back to my mom. "We worked on this the night you had to work late, and Max came over to keep me company."

It's a photo album, covered in velvet and filled with pictures of me, of Max, and of my mom, Max, and me all together.

My mom looks at it and her eyes start to tear again.

"Cry baby," I say.

"My baby," she says, hugging me.

"I'm not a baby anymore," I remind her.

"You'll always be my baby," she says.

"Mom," I say.

She hugs me again and then Max says, "Now for your present."

He picks it up and brings it over to me.

It looks heavy the way he's carrying it.

I reach for it.

"Let's put it on the table," Max says. "It'll be safer that way."

I, Amber Brown, have no idea what it is.

It's a kind of big box, one that Max had hidden in a small suitcase.

It's the first time that I've seen it.

Maybe it's the computer game thing that I asked for.

I want to shake it, but he's said to be careful so I am.

I just tip it a little.

It's very heavy.

I rip off the wrapping and open the box.

Inside the present is wrapped in a green garbage bag, like the ones that I used to wrap Justin and Danny's presents.

It's a ball.

It's a bowling ball.

It's a pink glitter bowling ball.

And my name is engraved on it . . . .

I turn it around. "There are no holes."

Max laughs. "It's a new way of bowling."

I look at him.

"Joke," he says. "We'll take it over to the sports shop and they'll drill holes in it that will be perfect for your fingers."

I hug the bowling ball.

"It's got to have a name," I say.

We start to think of names for the bowling ball. Split. Spare. Rover. Spot. Turkey. The Pink Comet. Destructo. The Avenger. Dropsy. The Ballamatic.

Finally, I think of one that I like. "It's called B.B., short for bowling ball . . . . so it will always be my B.B."

"And you will always be my baby," my mom says.

I cross my eyes at her.

"Max, thank you so much," I say. "Could I borrow that suitcase to keep B.B. in?"

He nods and smiles. "Okay . . . but something tells me that tomorrow when we light the candles there just might be something to keep that in."

"A bowling ball bag?" I ask. "Is it a pink glitter one?"

Max shrugs. "You'll see tomorrow."

"Oh no." I remember. "Tomorrow I'm going to be with my dad."

Actually, I, Amber Brown, have been looking forward to going over to my dad's house and seeing all of the things that we picked out.

This is my weekend with Dad, our time to be together before Christmas.

This will be my first time to stay over in my dad's and my house.

But I also want to be together with Mom and Max, and not just because of my bowling bag present.

I really like celebrating Hanukkah with Max . . . . and not just because of the presents.

Mom and Max and me. Dad and me.

I can't be in both places at the same time.

This is not easy.

And it's really just beginning.

It's going to be like this for the rest of my kid life.

I, Amber Brown, think about this.

I will probably have to be split like this forever.

Even when I am a grown-up.

I will always have to make choices.

Yikes! Double yikes.

It's weird.

In some ways, my life is better since my parents got divorced.

In some ways, it's harder.

But this is my life, and I've got to try to make it work out.

"Never mind," my mom says. "When you come back on Sunday, it will still be Hanukkah . . . . and we'll celebrate it then."

"And you will get your purple glitter bowling bag then," Max says, and then covers his mouth. "Ooops."

"Not very good at keeping secrets, are we???!!!!" my mom says, putting her arm around his waist.

He shakes his head and grins.

I think about my pink glitter bowling ball and my purple glitter bowling bag.

I may not be the best bowler in the league, but I will certainly be the most colorful.

And I, Amber Brown, love being colorful.

Chapter Fourteen

"Wow!" I say. "Dad, my room looks terrific."

He grins. "It does, doesn't it? It was amazing. One day the furniture was delivered . . . and the next day, four guys arrived from the company I called and in a few hours they assembled everything."

I look around my room.

There are two bureaus, a wardrobe closet, a desk, and a chair.

"Hooks are on the wall. The rug is on the floor. Curtains are hung." My dad points things out. "I did all of that. I also hung the shower curtain in your bathroom and put away all of the linens and the kitchen stuff."

"Wow," I say again. "You did all of that."

He grins. "Well, most of it. Mrs. Garfield, who cleans the Marshalls' house, helped me. She'll be working for us too."

"That means I won't have to make my bed?" I ask.

"No," he answers. "She'll be here only one day a week. You make your own bed, except for the day that she's working here."

"Shucks," I say.

My dad sits down on the office chair. "Amber, how are we going to work out your clothes? Do you want to bring some of them over here? That way you won't have to carry a suitcase to school on afternoons that you will be coming over to my house after you've been staying at your mother's."

I, Amber Brown, haven't thought about that. "I don't know. I'll talk to Mom."

He nods. "Okay . . . . and as for Christmas, I will give you a gift certificate to a department store, and you and your mom can go shopping for clothes for you."

I wonder if Mom will want to shop for stuff that will be staying in my Dad's house.

I just don't know.

I guess that my dad doesn't either because he says, "I can have Brenda Ambersit one day and take you shopping."

"Great," I say.

"Actually, I'm not so sure that's a good idea," he says.

"But it's your idea," I remind him.

"You won't end up dressing like Brenda?" He shakes his head. "She's a very nice person, but she has very strange taste."

"You mean like the things she's wearing today?" I say, remembering what she looked like when we came into the house and saw Polly and Brenda heading out the door.

Brenda had on a black skirt with a pink poodle on it over her leggings . . . . . and she was wearing a black T-shirt that says "Retro lives."

I, Amber Brown, have no idea who Retro is or where he, she, or it lives, but I thought that Brenda looked really great. I especially loved her pink high top sneakers and her lacy black and pink socks.

"I liked what Polly was wearing," I say, remembering Polly's black leggings and long turquoise sweater. "Maybe Brenda and Polly and I can go shopping together."

I wonder how I, Amber Brown, would look dressed up like Brenda, but don't tell my father that.

"Great idea," my dad says. "After Christmas, I'll send the three of you shopping . . . . and I'll treat everyone to lunch."

"Great." I think of all of the things that I can get.

There are some definite pluses to being a shared custody kid, even though this whole thing still makes me a little nervous.

"Amber. Mr. Brown," Savannah yells down from upstairs. "Is it okay if I come downstairs?"

"Yes," my dad and I yell at the same time.

"Pinkies," I say to my dad, holding up my pinky.

We link pinkies.

My dad starts to laugh. "Amber, the other day at work, my boss and I said the same thing at the same time and I yelled 'Link Pinkies.' I was very embarrassed."

I giggle. "What did your boss say? Did he think you are weird?"

My dad continues to laugh. "Actually, he

has a six-year-old daughter who makes him do it everytime they say something at the same time. So, he just linked pinkies."

Savannah and Dylan come running into the room.

They are really laughing.

They are holding something behind their backs.

"Guess," Dylan yells. "You've got to guess what we have."

I hate this game right now.

I like to HAVE someone else have to guess, but I don't like it when I have to be the guesser.

"You'll never guess." Dylan is jumping up and down.

Even more than having to guess, I hate being told that I'll never guess.

Finally, Dylan pulls something out from behind his back.

It's a lollipop, attached to the back half of a rubber rat.

Savannah has one that is a lollipop, attached to the back half of a rubber frog.
Gross. Really gross.

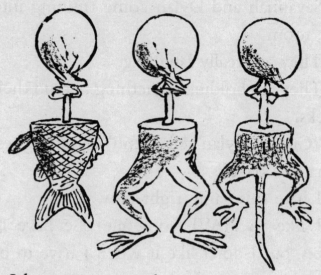

I have to get one!

"Merry Christmas early," Savannah says,
handing me a badly wrapped present. "Since
you aren't going to be here until after Christmas, we're giving this to you early."

It's a lollipop, with the back half of a rubber fish on it.

I really like it.

"Thank you," I say.

We all put the lollipops in our mouths and look like we have a fish, a frog, and a rat coming out of our mouths.

It's truly disgusting . . . and I really, really like it.

Something tells me that I'm really going have fun living in the same house with the Marshalls.

Chapter Fifteen

Dear Amber,

Surprise . . . . a Christmas card from your old friend, Justin Daniels. (Remember me??????) Mom said I should write to you. (You know that I hate to write. I wish that you still lived next door . . . . even though the boys around here *really* tease if a boy is friends with a girl . . . but we would be friends anyway . . . you're still the same . . . you don't do any-thing dumb like collect Barbie dolls or Beanie Babies, do you????)

The package from you and your
mom just arrived at our house . . . .
but mom said that we can't open it
until Christmas . . . . but even
wrapped, Danny and I have figured
out what you sent us. (We've been
bouncing the wrapped presents from
you around . . . . the bows came off
but it still looks good.) Anyway, we
hope that we are right about what's
in there . . . . and that it is unbreak-
able . . . . or my mom is going to be
really mad at us.

Only two more days until Christmas. . . . I can't wait.

Well, Merry Christmas and Happy
New Year.

Justin

P.S. My parents said that as one of my Christmas presents, I'm going to get a gift certificate to go away to camp this summer. Why don't you ask your parents if you can go too?

Chapter Sixteen

Dear Justin,

Finally, FINALLY, a letter from you!

I am soooooooo glad.

Actually, your Christmas card arrived right after Christmas. (Do you still turn your homework assignments in late??????)

A late Merry Christmas and an almost Happy New Year to you! (And Happy Hanukkah to you even though you don't celebrate it

. . . . . I do now . . . . . . and actually I think it's great to know about everyone's holidays . . . . next year I'm going to learn all about Kwanza.)

There is so much to tell you . . . . but I'm getting ready to return to my mom's and my house. (I'm at my dad's and my house right now.)

I live in two houses now . . . . . it's not always easy.

Sometimes I want to wear something, and it's at the other house.

Sometimes I want to finish reading a book, and it's at the other house.

Sometimes when I'm with my dad, I get homesick for my mom.

Sometimes when I'm with my mom, I get homesick for my dad.

. . . . And when I'm at one house and not the other, I wonder what

I'm missing at the house that I am not at.

Phew.

But I am definitely glad that my dad has moved back.

He's really sorry that he left, but we've talked about that . . . and I understand it a little better. (I wish that I didn't have to think about things like my parents' breakup and how they felt afterwards and why they did the things they do . . . . but I do, especially with my father.) Sometimes all of this makes me feel more grown-up than I want to be . . . but what the heck!

At my dad's house, there is a family that lives upstairs.

I think that you would really like the boy, Dylan . . . . . he's a couple of years older than us . . . . but he's funny a lot of the time. (When he's not being a pain.) Yesterday, he put half of a plastic rat under my pillow so that when I went to bed and pulled back the covers, there it was. (My screaming scared everyone in the house . . . . everyone but Dylan, that is!!!!!!!) He's a real trickster . . . and a pain, sometimes . . . . but I think that the two of you would really get along.

Guess what!?!? My ears are pierced!!! I did it without my mom's permission . . . I know, Bad Amber! You thought that my ears would have to be closed up . . . . . . or, even worse, kept open, OR that I could only wear Barney or Barbie earrings. BUT that didn't happen. I had to repay my dad for the piercing, pay if they got infected (they haven't), and I can only use the starter pair until I am twelve. I know . . . you, Justin Daniels, are saying, "Girl stuff. Piercing your ears. Yuck!" But it is important to me.

There's lots more going on . . . . but I know that you don't like to talk seriously, so I talk to Brandi and Kelly about a lot of stuff . . . and now I can also talk to Brenda, my Ambersitter . . . . and to Polly and Savannah, the other two kids who live upstairs.

I know that you hate when I say things that sound "mushy," but I still miss you lots . . . . and I think it's a great idea for both of us to go to the same camp this summer. I'm going to BEG my parents to let me go.

So, I hope that you have a Happy

New Year . . . that lots of good and interesting things happen. (And when is your new baby brother or sister going to be born????)

I wish you a Happy New Year . . . And I wish me one, too.

Love,

Amber

ABOUT THE AUTHOR

PAULA DANZIGER loves to write, and most of all, she loves to write for and about kids. She has written more than thirty books about characters who seem so real that readers really want to know them.

Amber Brown is one of these beloved characters—and she's funny, a little messy, and a very good friend.

Paula Danziger lives in Woodstock, New York; New York City; and London. And she loves pinball.